Get the R

Written by Alex Lane
Illustrated by Sholto Walker

OXFORD
UNIVERSITY PRESS

Rat!
Get the rat!

It is on the rug!

It is not the rat.
It is a sock!

Get the rat!
It is in the cup!

It is not the rat.

It is on his hat!

Get the rat!

It is not the rat.

It is a mess.

Bug!
Get the bug!

Retell the story

Once upon a time...

The end.